Illustrated by Jared Lee

A HIPPOPOTAMUS
ATE THE TEACHER!

By Mike Thaler

AN AVON CAMELOT BOOK

To all my teachers past and present

A HIPPOPOTAMUS ATE THE TEACHER is an original publication of
Avon Books. This work has never before appeared in book form.

AVON BOOKS
A division of
The Hearst Corporation
1790 Broadway
New York, New York 10019

First Camelot Printing, September 1981

CAMELOT TRADEMARK REG. U.S. PAT. OFF. AND IN
OTHER COUNTRIES, MARCA REGISTRADA, HECHO EN
U.S.A.

Printed in the U.S.A.

BAN   15   14   13   12

One day our teacher, Ms. Jones,
took us to the zoo.

She showed us the monkeys,

the tigers,

and the kangaroo.

Then she showed us the hippopotamus.

But she leaned too close to the rail
to feed it a peanut

and she fell in

and the hippopotamus ate her!

"Oh my!" we all cried. We went to the zoo
keeper and told him, "The hippopotamus just
ate our teacher."
"Oh my!" said the zoo keeper.

He went to the zoo director.
"The hippopotamus just ate their teacher."
"Oh my!" said the zoo director.

We went to the hippopotamus.

The zoo director opened up the hippopotamus's mouth and we all looked in. But we couldn't see anything.

Then all of a sudden a voice came from deep inside the hippopotamus. "All right class, it's time to go," said the voice.
It was Ms. Jones!

"Line up and hold hands," said the voice from
inside the hippopotamus. So we did.

"Follow me back to the bus," said the voice.
So we did.

Then the whole class rode back to school with the hippopotamus.

The other teachers were very surprised
when we all arrived.

The principal was very surprised also.

But we explained it to him.

So the next day the hippopotamus taught our class.

It taught us math

and history

and geography.

It read us stories.

All the other kids thought the hippopotamus was great. They looked in the windows and peeked in the doors. But as time went on we began to miss Ms. Jones.

It was hard to hug the hippopotamus
and we couldn't sit on its lap.

So one day in the middle of a history lesson we all grabbed the hippo and turned it upside down.

Then we shook it

till Ms. Jones fell out.

"Well class," she said. "Back to your seats."

"Any questions?" she smiled,
adjusting her glasses.